SEVEN POUNDS OF POTATOES PLEASE

In the mid 1970s Sheila and John, together with their large family, leave their smallholding in the Weald of Kent to take on a new challenge – a small village store in the West Country. Life at the Crossroads Store, selling everything from fruit and veg to buckets and torches, is never dull, and some of their customers are decidedly eccentric! The work is hard and the hours long, but they soon become part of the community – exploring the beautiful countryside and accumulating even more pets, including Torty, the disappearing tortoise. However, as their older children begin to leave home their thoughts return to Kent...

SEVEN POUNDS OF POTATOES PLEASE

Seven Pounds Of Potatoes Please

by

Sheila Newberry

Dales Large Print Books
Long Preston, North Yorkshire,
BD23 4ND, England.

British Library Cataloguing in Publication Data.

Newberry, Sheila
Seven pounds of potatoes please.

A catalogue record of this book is available from the British Library

ISBN 978-1-84262-705-1 pbk

Published in Large Print 2009 by arrangement with Sheila Newberry, care of Judith Murdoch Literary Agency

Dales Large Print is an imprint of Library Magna Books Ltd.

Printed and bound in Great Britain by
T.J. (International) Ltd., Cornwall, PL28 8RW

Introduction

'What happened next?' readers of *Knee Deep in Plums* often ask.

Plums was a memoir of the happy days when our large family lived on a small-holding in the Weald of Kent, from the 1960s into the '70s.

To continue: in the middle '70s, we left our orchard paradise for pastures new, a small village in the West Country, to an area where we had spent several adventurous holidays under canvas. We were now the excited (if naive) owners of the Crossroads Stores, which fronted an old house, full of character, wattle and daub, with creaking floors but many rooms for the family to rattle around in. Out the back there was a rusting paraffin tank, a redundant privy with honeysuckle round the door and a ramshackle barn, full of secrets… The garden was enclosed by a crumbling dry stone wall. In the front courtyard there was a mounting block for horses, which intrigued the girls, who were looking forward to gallops on the moor. There was an abundance of riding stables round and about.

The children who were young and such fun in the *Plums* days were growing up fast, one after the other. Our eldest son was working away from home, but joined us at weekends, the three girls were involved with A levels, pursuing further studies at college, and working in a TV studio in town before going on to art college. The middle three boys were in their teens, strapping blond lads, much involved with sport. These seven featured prominently in *Plums* – they might prefer to tell their own stories now!

I have heeded the mild complaints of the youngest, Katharine and Matthew, who appeared in the final chapters of *Plums*. *Seven Pounds of Potatoes Please* is, therefore, dedicated to Kate and Matt, (Katy and

Maff as we called them then) with my love. At the time we moved they were just five and three years old, and golden-haired, but Maff had all the curls! She was so petite, he was already a head taller than her, and they were a real double act.

I hope you will enjoy reading about John, me, and our young pickles, with the girls drifting in and out dreamily, in short skirts, smock frocks and white boots, with long hair and beads; catching a glimpse or two of the boys with the dogs and an often deflated football up on Little Moor. You'll see me, too, out of shop hours, in floaty Madras cotton dresses or purple Crimplene trousers and geometric patterned tops – I'd had enough of smocks to last me over the last two decades! When I wore my neat nylon overall behind the counter, my own long hair was restrained in Indian braids. Even John had a pink brocade shirt and a maroon kipper tie – though he says he can't recall it! I should reassure readers that this is as 'hippy' as we got!

Now you are about to make the acquaintance of some *special* customers whom we will never forget…

P.S. I just discovered that tie lurking in the wardrobe after all these years!

One

Seven Pounds of Potatoes Please

Christmas Day, the first in our new home. We sat in happy anticipation round our Victorian Loo table, which rested on a pedestal embellished with lion claws. When we were first married, John and I purchased this for ten shillings from a local junk shop, and bowled it home upended, precariously along the pavement, as we couldn't fit it into our motorcycle sidecar. The table was faded and scratched then, but John lovingly French-polished the rosewood top and it was now a treasured possession.

The girls had laid the table with our wedding silver and the frosted pink glass water set. The turkey, basted to perfection, sat on a huge dish in the centre. The splendid home cooked ham, coated in golden breadcrumbs, was adorned with a paper frill. Steam wafted lazily from the vegetable dishes. We'd been cutting a cross in the stem of the sprouts while awash with Christmas wrapping paper. John was about to carve the first succulent slices on to the top plate of the pile, when we became aware of a strange noise – our dining room opened directly on to the courtyard outside the shop, and something was being pushed stealthily through the front door letter box. Could this be a belated Christmas parcel? We stared, mesmerised as a long, dun-coloured, folded object appeared, then plopped onto the mat. I recognised it immediately – I encountered that old oilskin bag daily on the counter!

Cautiously, I opened the door and glanced up and down the street. It was deserted. Probably the whole village was sitting down to Christmas dinner, I thought. I closed the door, bag in hand, wondering why whoever brought it had disappeared in haste.

'Oh, no,' I exclaimed, 'surely Mrs Dean

doesn't want a delivery today…' There was a pencilled note inside, written on an old envelope: It read, Seven Pounds of Potatoes Please (my daughter's had a baby.)

'We're closed,' John said firmly. 'We stayed open until almost seven last night – remember? She had plenty of time to do her shopping then.'

'But – her daughter's had a baby…' I said. 'She was probably up most of the night.'

'So were we,' he reminded me. 'We had all our own Christmas preparations still to do… Eat your dinner first. Surely they can wait?'

'They're obviously out of potatoes,' I insisted. 'It won't take me long to weigh them, then one of the boys can run round to the Dean's house with the bag.'

'Aw, mum!' the boys sighed reproachfully. 'We're hungry!'

My dinner plate went in the Rayburn, while I hurried up the hill with the heavy bag, still wearing my golden paper crown, to the row of old farm cottages on the edge of the council estate, where the Dean family lived. Mrs Dean, a tiny woman with a permanently worried expression, appeared at the door with an apron over her nightgown, and brand new Christmas slippers. A couple of her smaller girls clutched her apron strings. Somewhere a baby gave a plaintive cry. A strapping girl clad in just a brief top, revealing long, bare legs, came out from the back room, pushed past her mother and pounded up the steep stairs, to answer the call. There was no sign of the reclusive Mr Dean. I wondered if he actually existed. We'd heard he was retired – he was certainly retiring – had we almost met him today? As the rest of the family were not yet dressed, it seemed likely that he had left the bag.

'Thanks, love – we wasn't aware my daughter was even expecting – quite a night, I tell you… Get peeling them spuds you lot! Merry Christmas!' The door closed in my face.

'Bet she didn't pay for the potatoes,' John said.

'Think of it as a special delivery!' I replied.

We left our old home on a perfect summer's day the previous June. Our goods and chattels had been packed and removed the day before. I had supervised this as best I could, as John was summoned to the last day stock keeping at the shop, and wasn't due back until the early hours. We slept for the last time in Crabapple Cottage, lying on the floor in our sleeping bags. The kindly removal men had been super efficient and packed everything in sight, including my shoes and the Swan Vestas. When John came wearily in, we tried to strike a solitary match on the wooden boards to brew tea on the camping stove, to no avail.

At first light, we were thankful to rise and flex aching joints. We ate a picnic lunch in the orchard, as we had the day we arrived there. The chickens, including dear Henrietta, the bun-snatcher, and other livestock had not been replaced, the old dogs had gone, now we had a lively, tiny Jack Russell pup named Florence; but Tiger, the ancient ginger tom cat was around – but where? We searched in all his favourite places, but he was not to be found.

A kind neighbour told us not to worry, she would look out for him, feed him, and despatch him to us by train. We learned later that another neighbour (remember long, lanky Chas, another unexpected child, whose standard charge for services rendered, was five bob? Well, this was his mother who much preferred cats to children) had enticed him into her shed, and hidden him until after we departed.

John's family joined us in the orchard for the picnic and we looked around us at the trees and back at the old house with its now blank, reproachful windows. One thing we were sure of, we would never forget this place – although we didn't realise then, that it would always mean 'home' to all of us…

'Don't look back,' we said to one and another as we drove away in our Commer Minibus. But I know I was crying, and I couldn't understand why.

Two

From the Crossroads

It was like stepping back in time – the village appeared to be just as it had been for generations. From the shop, the road wound down lazily over a hump-backed bridge. There was another big house attached to ours, where nice middle-aged Martha lived alone, now her parents were gone. She played the organ in the church and was the school cook. She also practised on a harmonium in her bedroom, the other side of the wall from the girls, and snatches of rousing hymns entertained them, amplified by the joint chimney breast. The girls sang loudly to let her know she was disturbing their slumbers, but then she pulled all the stops out, obviously appreciating their involvement.

Next, there was a row of two-up, two-down cotts, where most of our regular customers lived, conveniently opposite the pub, which we gathered was also the working men's club.

On the same side as the cotts was the primary school, which until about five years ago, we learned, had a handful of pupils, an ageing head teacher who plied the cane, and with the furnishings of the 1880s, when it was founded. Then, on the plateau of the steep hill along which the bus ran morning and evening, to the village, turning at the crossroads, a large, posh estate of houses was built, which attracted affluent strangers with cars who commuted to town to work. These newcomers didn't deign to shop at the stores, but the school was a different matter; they saw its potential. By the time we arrived, there was a young, enthusiastic headmaster, modern equipment and, amazingly, a swimming pool. The money had been raised by the parents of the new intake of pupils. Katy would shortly be in her element as a new pupil and enthusiastic water baby with floats.

Turn the corner across the road at this point and you were going uphill again, past a little front room post office run by a brother and sister who viewed us with suspicion, and there was the church, seemingly in the middle of nowhere, silhouetted against the horizon, where the crows nested. Most of the villagers were chapel, and the parson, known as Bouncy Ball, his surname, and yes, it described his shape, met most of his flock in the pub, rather than in the pews. He was well-liked, but his congregation was on occasion, just the church warden and grave digger. Once, it was only John, me, and a stranger. The parson disappeared mid-service, we sat on in apprehensive silence, but eventually, we went home. We heard later that he had totally forgotten we were there...

He did indeed bounce home to the vast, chilly rectory... His cassock was fastened with safety pins, and we treasure a letter from my dad to the big girls, which suggests, 'Why don't you sew him up with your needle and thread?'

Little Moor Road was more a lane, branching off from the crossroads in the opposite direction to the snooty new estate and downhill all the way. You had to watch out for the cattle grids. Here were all the big houses behind high walls with iron gates. Retired Colonels and their like lived here, and did not mix with the hoi polloi. The moor tumbled green and verdant down to a bubbling stream and beyond that was a lovely old farmhouse. Miss Dingle was in charge of the dairy and the Jersey cows – her clotted cream was much coveted. We were privileged to receive a carton of it each week, which we paid for, of course, but it built up in the fridge. You can't eat this luxury food every day.

The view from our shop window was as idyllic. Another stream splashed clear water where children paddled, and rising above this low point was a meadow with two or three gentle cows with following calves.

These were the pets of the neighbours across the road, a kindly couple, the Trews, who made us welcome. Mrs T had only one son, whom we never met, and she shared her home with her daughter-in-law Dee, an attractive young woman, and also an adopted daughter, Anne, who had cerebral palsy. Anne communicated with us in her own way, a delightful, happy girl. She worked in a sheltered workshop and liked to come into the shop after she received her modest wage packet to choose a small gift for her foster mother and a mixed bag of her favourite sweets.

Anne, we learned, was one of twins, born prematurely. Her young mother couldn't cope with two babies, one of whom was handicapped. When her grandmother, who remained in touch with Anne, heard that she was to be placed in an institution, she brought the tiny baby wrapped in a shawl, to her friend Mrs Trew, who had always wanted a daughter. Although Anne was in and out of hospital most of her young life, undergoing operations, Mrs Trew didn't falter in her devotion to the girl, and it was obviously reciprocated.

Mrs Trew was tall and slender, with striking auburn hair, blue eyes and pale skin; her husband was obviously of village stock, being short, with black hair, swarthy skin and brown eyes. Talking of eyes, it was rather disconcerting to notice how many of the older male locals had one good eye and one 'wonky one', so we assumed they were all related… 'Everyone shopped here 'til a few years ago,' Mrs Trew observed. 'The old owners sold everything from corsets to corn plasters. Not much money passed hands – people paid in kind, like the odd poached salmon or half a pig. Then when the folk afore you come along, they only lasted a year, they altered everything. They don't take to change round here, m'dear. Most went up the hill to the Co-op. Mind you,' she added to soften the bombshell, for we'd thought we were taking on a thriving business, 'the shop is cleaner and brighter, with much more variety. It's good to have a family here again. If they take to you they'll be back…'

Three

We'll Fill the Shelves
(whether you want it, or not)

To our eyes, the shop was attractively laid out, with labelled shelving, cold cabinets and a huge modern freezer, with frozen peas and fish fingers alongside much requested bright pink sausages and yellow dairy ice-cream.

We had a splendid bacon and ham slicer. One of our most urgent tasks was to clean this, after our arrival, for the previous owners' Persian cats had obviously groomed themselves in close proximity to the slicer and it was gummed up with fur. The thought crossed our minds that the cats had enjoyed licking the blades... It was unfortunate that the preparation area was in the kitchen beyond the shop, and when we had to leave that unattended, we worried, with reason, what was happening during our brief absence… On our return, it was to cast an eye over the packets of tea, or cans of baked beans, to check if pyramids were in danger of toppling.

The shop was supposed to be self-service but most like Mrs Dean, ignored the wire baskets and filled their own bags. There was the odd 'forgetful' customer who disappeared out of the door, bypassing the up to date electric till, which necessitated a breathless dash outside by whoever was serving and a polite 'reminder' to pay up, please – however, we soon discovered that most of our customers while very poor, were honest. It was a minority, mostly incomers, as Mrs Trew told us firmly, to whom getting one over new shopkeepers was a way of life. We had to show them we knew what they were up to. A strategically placed mirror helped somewhat, alongside the five bottles of expensive His'n'hers perfume – six had been counted on the stock list, but over the night before our arrival, one had mysteriously vanished. (We never sold any at all, but two bottles were missing after the final stocktaking. The same culprit, was our rueful guess.)

The counter guarded the tobacco and cigarettes on the wall unit behind – no self service allowed in that respect. Also out of reach was a card of sachets of saffron. Despite its luxury price, no celebration cake was made in these parts without a few strands, and the taste made rich fruit cakes even more special.

There was a newspaper stand, and we whittled down the contents after we noticed that most of the wonky-eyed brigade were more interested in stealthily riffling the pages of top shelf lurid magazines, than buying fresh Cornish pasties (giant-sized) and stale chocolate sponges with a tinge of green 'decoration', which we'd inherited, piled high on the cake and biscuits shelf. We shortly disposed of the services of the

Cadbury Cake man and purchased fresh cakes from the wholesalers.

We were supplied with local produce by those who assured us that they had been doing this for so many years, they could judge exactly the amounts needed. We were grateful for their expertise in the beginning, but very soon twigged that most were pulling a fast one.

Tinkerbelle, we dubbed the thin man with oiled back black hair and pencil moustache, who supplied the stocking stand with his Belle tights, pop socks and sheer nylons. He came every month and counted up how many we had sold – we could never prove that his sums added up, because he always slid sideways into the shop at a busy time, assuring us in a stage whisper: 'Don't worry, I can manage – I'll give you the total when you're free…' Tinkerbelle was obsequious, I thought. He asked me, the first time he called, 'May I speak to your mother, dear?' When I told him that I was the co-owner of the shop, emphasising 'with my husband', he was unabashed. 'You look so young,' he gushed.

Tinkerbelle's tights often laddered after one wearing, and we were resigned to replacing them for customers. As Mrs Dean said, 'Can't you get the lisle ones any more? They lasted for ever.' (She pronounced lisle as 'lissel'.) This was true, I thought, seeing wrinkled tan stockings on a very ancient customer, who commented, regarding the Belle stand, 'Them flimsy things show all your varicosities'.

The pasties and a weekly batch of farm-house crusty bread were made by a farmer's wife with a heavy hand and rolling pin. The filling in the pasties was tasty and well-seasoned, but there was the traditional wide, crimped edging to enable a hungry worker with grubby hands to grasp the solid pastry, bite into the middle, then discard the crust. Our worry was that those who placed a regular order, sometimes omitted to collect on the day and then refused to pay for 'stale goods.' We ended up having to eat the surplus, because *we* certainly were expected to stump up, in advance. I'd never had a weight problem until then, but eating the left-overs set me on the road to Weight Watchers.

The sausage man, beaming and red-cheeked, also delivered great tubs of ice-cream, I suspect some of the same ingredients were involved. The sausages as I said were a lurid pink, fat and slippery in great ropes, which the sausage man festooned in loops taking up half the freezer. You could request chipolatas, but they were all jumbo size. They were obviously a village staple food and we often sold out.

The fruit and veg man proudly presented items grown on his own allotment. Everything he grew was enormous and we knew he had won prizes at flower shows, but big is not always tender, is it? When customers asked for a pound of anything, like leeks or swedes (always called turnips, while cauliflowers were known as 'broccola') they usually received a single vegetable – the range also included an onion like a beach ball, or a carrot that no bunny could manage to nibble. There was good earth caked under Les's finger nails, proving things were fresh-dug. You had to watch out for caterpillars in the cabbages, and wrigglers in the pea pods, and you needed a cleaver to dice the carrots. We sold more of the latter than any other vegetable, a good many to a neighbour of Mrs Dean's, whose complexion turned bright orange, so we gathered she was addicted to them. We learned to have only a couple on display at a time. We were forced to tell this poor woman that carrots were in short supply due to – er – carrot fly...

What else did we sell in the shop? Plastic buckets and bowls, torches, bandages and yes, corn plasters, milk and yoghurts, toys, sweets in jars, chocolate bars, plus trays of penny candy on the counter, for the little ones to choose from. Occasionally, these were dribbled on, when a mother held her toddler over the dolly-mixtures while she picked out the jelly ones.

Other commodities were bought regularly by John from the wholesalers on the outskirts of town. We priced it all carefully according to the 'Grocer's bible', but our customers could always sniff out a bargain. When we sold a month's supply of loo rolls in a day, it was time to re-check the price, too late. We also learned to our cost that when we obliged by getting in a special item, the customer who wanted this so urgently, no longer required it, and probably nobody else did, either.

My unfavourite task was to fill the various containers presented daily for a 'pint of paraffin.' It appeared most folk cooked on an oil stove. Toddy, a big lad, with a blond cowlick of hair, aged 14, well mannered, who caught the school bus with our boys each morning, often scarpered home, after registration and usually turned up when there was a lull in the shop and John was collecting goods in town or out delivering to a farm. I asked, 'Couldn't you wait until my husband gets back?' but he said quickly,

'Mum says she needs it *now!* I'll mind the shop, Missis…'

That darn tank produced a thin trickle, and I agonised over what pilfering could be going on while I tried to fill a lemonade bottle, with a fervent little prayer.

When I returned, Toddy was always leaning innocently against the door, and nothing appeared to have been disturbed.

'I didn't let nobody in,' he said virtuously. 'They all went away.'

Thanks Toddy, I thought. 'Here you are,' I said feebly, handing over the bottle. I couldn't help having a soft spot for Toddy despite my suspicions. I also knew he'd be back when the bottle was empty to claim the refund. The Corona man would not be pleased at the whiff of paraffin, but he'd continue to fill *his* allotted shelf with Dandelion and Burdock.

Four

Early Doors

The newspapers arrived with a thud before dawn – thrown at the front door by a passing van. At five-thirty a.m. John stood, yawning, marking them with his pencil, and folding them ready for delivery. We had our own family paper boys, of course, who pedalled cheerfully up and down hill, hoping the guard dogs kennelled outside the big houses were still asleep, but we shortly heard a crescendo of barking, in Little Moor Road.

Still, that was preferable to the irate retired naval commander, who only came in the shop to complain that if the staff of a certain broadsheet were on strike, thus no paper, what were *we* were going to do about it? We also discovered early on that some people don't like to pay for newspapers *after* they've read 'em. Bills were often queried.

From 6 to 7, I was busy with breakfast, and the girls kindly encouraged the young ones to wash and get dressed. I cooked on the Rayburn in the kitchen, and family soon appeared at the appetising smell of frying bacon. As always, we 'all pulled together.'

We officially opened the shop at 8 a.m. Unofficially, I listened out for the hacking coughs of farm workers out there in the still dark, misty morning, plus the damp and cold from late September until Spring. The amount of wet weather in the west during these months, came as quite a shock to us, although it was certainly not as chilly as it was in the south-east.

As I laid the first rashers of bacon in our huge frying pan, there would come a tapping on the shop door. Sighing, I went through to unbolt the door, but left the sign at CLOSED.

More coughing, a wheeze or two, then the

early workers, wound round with scarves, wearing fingerless gloves and woolly caps – I never knew their names – requested, 'A packet of green papers, Missus, please, and half an ounce of the strongest...' They rolled the first fag of the day as they stood outside for a moment, and the lovely smell of bacon was eclipsed by that of rank tobacco. Although, as a non-smoker, I wished we didn't have to stock this commodity, I appreciated that these, often elderly men needed their smokes to cope with all the hard graft ahead.

We had a potent remedy for coughs by the till: lozenges which had been formulated for deep sea fishermen and these proved a best seller, too. John tried one for a sore throat one night in bed, went to sleep, and woke in the morning to find the lozenge glued to the roof of his mouth. He complained about the taste for several days, but it did the trick.

The before-hours customers kept arriving, all through breakfast. It was a tradition we couldn't break. I'd be flipping the eggs in the pan, and there would be yet another knock, more timorous this time. I could guess who. 'Mrs Diddley – can someone finish the eggs off?' I asked.

I was right – it was Elsie Diddley from the cotts. She was shrouded in an old overcoat, but her faded fair hair was combed into a snood in the style of the '40s when she had been a pretty young girl, doing her bit for the war effort in a factory. Mrs D certainly didn't smell of His'n'Hers perfume – she absolutely reeked of bleach. She was the school cleaner. She got through about three large bottles of the stuff each week, which her poor, red hands bore testament to. I tried tactfully to suggest rubber gloves might help, but Mrs D shook her head. 'You got to get the feel of what you're doing,' she said, in her soft, almost inaudible voice. I could picture those hands scrubbing away in the toilet block, and winced to think how much they must pain her. She was one of several small, frail looking women locally who had produced large idle offspring on whom they appeared to wait hand and foot. Cuckoos in the nest, I thought compassionately.

At 7.30 a.m., the first bus was due at the crossroads. A minute or two before this, several women, including Mrs Trew's Dee, some with hair in curlers under turbans, arrived to buy their daily cigarettes, a newspaper and a bag of Everton mints. They had the best paid jobs, making wireless components in a factory. They would return that evening at 6 p.m. to knock on the shop door if we had actually closed on time, for 'sausages, m'dear, for tea. Quick to do: it's Bingo night in the village hall.' The Rev. Bouncy Ball had introduced this attraction, and was the caller. He also organised monthly discos in the hall, and the most requested record, which caused us to pull the covers over our heads in bed on a Saturday night, was *Vive Espana!*

The High School bus came at 8.15. The shop was now officially open at last, and John and I joined forces to control the influx of teenagers. Our lot escaped the back way, to be first in the queue at the bus stop, with a modest choc bar apiece for break time.

Katy and Maff sat on stools behind the counter, and were made a fuss of by Toddy's younger sister, a boisterous nine year old named Loretta, with freckles and a loud voice, who sometimes yelled out to John, 'You want to watch my brother, mister!'

The till rang incessantly, and we hoped the bus would arrive early so that the shop would empty in double quick time.

Just time for a reviving cup of tea, before it was time to walk Katy to school. Loretta would be sitting on our front wall, swinging her legs, waiting to accompany us, and to impart Toddy's latest misdemeanours.

'Mum said you just wait 'til Dad comes home, but Toddy knew he was safe, 'cos Dad was down the pub with his mates, and *he* was going to get it from Mum first, I reckon!' she said, adding, 'She forgot to give me 10p for the swimming today – could I borrow it from you, Katy's mum?' Of course, I obliged. Her mum was a large lady with a fierce expression, and always hard-up, but she made sure her family were well fed. Ten pence pieces were in short supply in her house, I guessed.

At the school gate, Loretta took Katy's little hand in hers. 'Don't worry, I'll look after you, and help you in the pool this afternoon. I'll mangle all the water out of your costume, when I do mine, eh?' She was the youngest in her family, but was a real little mother.

'I'm on poolside duty,' I told her. I wanted to be sure Katy was confident in the water, it wasn't the same as paddling in the sea, which she loved. I'd added my name to the parents' rota, for Wednesday afternoons, when we were open only half the day. I'd had plenty of experience with the portable pool in the orchard when the others were growing up. This was also an open-air pool, and two supervisors were required, facing each other on either side, one a parent and the other a qualified teacher/instructor, who was in charge.

I needn't have worried: there was Katy, already in the shallow end, when I hurried round to the school at 2.30. She looked so tiny, in her blue costume with a yellow sunflower on the front and her bathing cap. She took to swimming like a duck to water, with inflated armbands, and her chubby limbs flailing – within a week she could do a width, and float on her back. Maff watched from the side but shook his head when invited to join his sister in the water. He liked to weigh up things before he joined in, he still does. He was the responsible one of the two, even though he was younger. They balanced each other nicely.

'Watch me, Katy's mum! Watch me!' called Loretta, attempting to swim a length under water. I obliged, but I thought, her own mum is missing out – Loretta is sometimes a pain in the neck, but she's a real character! Not only did she later put Katy's costume through the wringer which had been presented to the school by Mrs Trew, kept on the step outside the boys' and girls' changing rooms, but she cheerfully stood there in her own dripping costume, a baggy navy blue one, obviously passed down by an older sibling, seeing to all the other children's swimming togs first, as they emerged in their dry clothing. Oh, we did like Loretta!

Five

Old cat, young dog, and roaming tortoise

A month elapsed before Tiger was located and sent by rail to be collected. John and the children met two trains before he finally turned up. He stepped, stiff-legged, out of the carrying basket on to the kitchen floor. He ignored the saucer of milk, the bowl of food, but he began his rumbling purr. He was lifted up, which he wouldn't have tolerated in his prime, and it was as if he weighed hardly anything at all. We stroked his faded ginger striped coat, and carried him to inspect the barn. This was more like it, we could tell, and he chose a cosy corner to sit and watch comings and goings. Unwisely, we decided to keep him safe indoors overnight. I even buttered his paws. The store room seemed a good place, with all the goods well off the floor. He was too arthritic to climb. However, he marked every corner of what we'd dubbed the dungeon, so like Mrs Diddley, we had cause to resort to bleach and a scrubbing brush. Tiger had always been an outside cat and was now too old to change his ways, we realised. He soon settled down to his mouse-patrol in the barn, and continued to regard little Florence, the Jack Russell pup, with his unblinking gaze. She was eager to be his buddy, but Tiger the once feral cat certainly wasn't about to permit to any familiarity.

The family persuaded us that we needed a canine pal for Florence. A bigger dog, perhaps. One or two dark-jowled men, observing her over the five-barred gate which closed off the back garden, had enquired slyly if they could buy Florence to use for hunting purposes – poaching, we thought was more it. When we declined, they went off, but we worried they might come back and take her anyway. Florence needed a protector!

We scoured the local ads and were struck by one which read:

OLD ENGLISH X
BORDER COLLIE PUPS – £20

We rang the number given, and were told there were just two left – a bitch which took after the mother, a collie, and a dog pup which was like its father, an old English sheepdog.

John recalled a dog from his childhood which had belonged to an elderly lady, Miss Moses, whom he had helped with hay-making during the war. 'He was a beautiful Old English – he was called Blue Billow,' he said.

'Dad – can we go and buy him today?' the family chorused. 'We want a Blue Billow, too!'

It was a Saturday – I said I could manage the shop – so they all piled into the minibus, plus Florence and drove off to Bodmin Moor.

I wish I had seen it myself, but I could picture the setting from their vivid description: dogs were everywhere, mostly collies, on moorland grazed by sheep. The dogs were atop grassy hillocks barking furiously. Chickens were flapping and scratching around. The farmhouse sat in a hollow below, near the road, where the minibus was parked. It had been quite a climb up the hill.

The pups were huddled together in a chicken coop, noses poking through the wire mesh. They were thin and shivering, and the dog pup was not the beautiful animal we had envisaged. He was still black and white, as Old English pups are until they grow a top grey coat. He had a whippy tail, but soulful eyes which seemed to plead: You're going to take me home, aren't you? His sister was already booked, just as well, as the family wouldn't have liked to leave her on her own.

Our third daughter, sixteen year old Ginge, now a tall girl with long chestnut hair and dark eyes, was great with animals. Florence, we accepted, was her special charge, although we all enjoyed our pet. Billow loved us indiscriminately. When he was out with the lads, he was 'one of the boys' – he joined in all the games, puncturing the football, but scoring many a goal. He swam with them in streams and in the sea, he was a real water dog, and he enjoyed shaking droplets all over anyone near by. He grew into a very handsome dog, resembling a bearded collie, with grey fur and a splendid, plumed tail. He had kind brown eyes under his fringe, and an amiable nature. However! He was quite an escape artist. He could clear a five barred gate in a graceful leap, and he was a would-be Romeo – he was drenched with the occasional pail of water, I'm afraid. But when he shook hands with you and put his nose on your feet when he sat snoozing beside you, well, you could forgive him anything. We were fortunate to have him for sixteen years.

Sadly, we only had little Florence for 2 years. She was run over by a farm tractor, poor Ginge was inconsolable. We were all very sad.

Matthew wanted a tortoise, and got his wish. The tortoise had a shiny, patterned shell, and fascinated his small owner, who looked after him well and offered him succulent lettuce leaves. He laughed out loud when Torty's head popped out from the shell and he nibbled his food.

Unfortunately, it appeared that Torty, like Billow, enjoyed going beyond the boundaries of the garden. Maff would run indoors to report: 'I can't find him, Mummy! He's disappeared.'

The first couple of times, I said, 'Well, he can't be far away – he's a tortoise and they are very slow, you know.'

We put up a notice in the shop window: TORTOISE MISSING. SMALL REWARD FOR HIS RETURN!

On each occasion, after a few hours, with the village children alerted, Torty was brought home. Toddy had found him, but was vague about exactly where. I indicated the chocolate section. 'Take your pick!'

'Cor, thanks Missus!' he beamed. 'Glad to help.'

Some rewards later our suspicions aroused, but unconfirmed, Loretta split on her brother.

'He nips in your garden, Katy's mum, and pinches 'im!' she said. 'That ain't right.'

'No – it – ain't – isn't,' I said, suppressing a wry smile.

I guess she told Toddy what she'd done, because the tortoise napping stopped. I didn't confront Toddy, because he knew that I knew, and that was enough. Anyway, as we had replaced the chocolate with a swizzle lolly of late, he probably reckoned it wasn't worth the bother.

However, this is not quite the end of this particular story…

'I found your tortoise – do you still give

rewards?' another lad asked diffidently. This was Wim, short for William I suppose, a shy and silent type as a rule, who seemed rather a loner. Another big boy with a tiny, energetic mother. Wim held out a tortoise which was Torty sized, but with a crack on the shell.

Oh dear, I thought, Torty has had a mishap! The larger reward seemed to be fitting, and Wim departed with his Mars bar, and a bemused expression. I bet he shared it with his little sister.

John examined the crack. It was obviously an old wound, healed over. He took the tortoise into the garden, only to discover what I should have checked before, that Torty was ambling around out there.

So a notice duly went up in the shop window:

TORTOISE FOUND (NOT OURS)
IF YOU HAVE LOST ONE, PLEASE
ASK IN SHOP.

So then there were two. Where Oisey came from remains a mystery.

Six

Concorde and Kites

We decided from our very first Sunday in the shop, that we would have to go out for the day if we were to avoid the taps on the door from the likes of Mrs Dean, requesting potatoes or Toddy, with another Corona bottle for paraffin, which had probably been 'lifted' from the crate put out for the Corona man on Fridays. This doubled the refund on the bottle!

We had the moor on our doorstep, where we enjoyed summer evening strolls before John settled to the shop accounts and the children to their homework, but on Wednesday afternoons, after they returned from school, we often drove a short distance to a magical place, which we fondly imagined was known to us exclusively. We had discovered by chance one day a crystal waterfall splashing into a rushing stream with stepping stones, and springy grass, nibbled by sheep, for ball games and picnic teas. We took our shoes off and cooled our toes in the spray.

On Sundays, we ventured further afield. Before our move we'd toured all round the lovely coast of Dorset, Devon and Cornwall during our camping holidays and were eager to re-visit two favourite places, one in Devon and the other in Cornwall.

The 70s were record summers for sunshine. We left home early in the morning, before the heat of the day, and returned when the temperature cooled, in the evening. Our minibus had a variety of seats, Sara sat in a single seat by the side door to control the entry and exit of her exuberant brothers – they sat together on a long seat facing a table, on which were spread comics, board games and their young brother's toy cars. I was on the opposite bench, with

Maff, ostensibly minding the boys, while, JP and Ginge (the only one to suffer travel sickness) were in the front with John.

Jo and Katy shared a seat behind Sara, and the dog fitted in where he saw a space. Although we no longer used the van for camping, alongside our big tent, we'd retained the stove at the rear, and the cupboard where we now stacked our bags and cold box full of food. We still liked to have a fresh brew of tea. The thunder box was also in its allotted spot, but as we were often reminded by John, who had to empty it, for 'emergency use only!'

It was an hour or so's drive to our chosen destination, along narrow lanes with fields either side protected by mossy dry stone walls.

Curious cows, with long flirty eyelashes regarded us over farm gates. A farm dog barked, and Billow pricked his ears. If we met a tractor, one or other of the vehicles would have to back up cautiously, sometimes for a mile or two, before a lay-by was reached. Like Gracie Fields, in an old film, I had seen at the local fleapit as a child, we loved to 'Sing as We Go.' Katy performed her party piece, 'Raindrops are falling on my head,' but it was, happily, that day, 'Blue Skies Smiling at Me.'

At last we came to the road which led down a steep incline to a field: private land, but limited parking permitted. We walked briskly across the grass – well Chris, Mike and Roger ran of course – inhaling the good sea air, carrying our towels, bathers and bags of items like suncream, calamine lotion, plasters, dog biscuits, bowls and bottles of water, plus books and sunglasses. John carried the food! At least the box would be lighter, going back.

The boys disappeared down the cliff path to the soft sand of the tidal estuary beach. Across the stretch of shimmering water there rose a green meadow, on which cattle grazed. At low tide you could walk to the other side, but had to take care not to be stranded there when the tide came in again.

There were outcrops of rock to sit on, to spread our towels and some flat enough for sun bathing. If the sun was too strong, we could retreat to where the cliff overhung and cast a welcome shade.

It really was a beautiful spot, and it was easy for me to relax and dream away the day, while the young ones napped on my lap, and the rest of the family dashed in and out of the water with Billow.

One afternoon, however, a coach load of trippers arrived to blast the air with music, and loud voices, with binoculars, which they trained not on the sea birds, or the pastoral scene across the water, but on our three pretty daughters, innocently sunbathing on the rocks in their bikinis.

Not wishing them to be embarrassed, we decided to drape our towels round our shoulders, go back to the van to get dressed and go in search of a shaded garden where we could treat ourselves to a cream tea. The family thought this was a splendid idea.

As always, the boys led the cavalcade, with

Billow dashing backwards and forwards, to make sure we were following. While the lads skirted the rowdy party, now unpacking their lunch, Billow had no such inhibitions: he bounded through the middle of them, scattering them with sand, and even as they shouted indignantly, he casually cocked his leg and peed over their sandwiches.

By unspoken, common consent, we thought it prudent to pretend he was a friendly dog who'd attached himself to us on the beach.

Vengeance was sweet.

We went by ferry from Plymouth to Cornwall, the young ones were as excited as if they were on a cruise! Then we drove on to a place with an Irish name – forgive me for not being specific! Maybe it has been 'discovered' in later years, but then it was not as well-known as the main resorts.

There we scrambled down a trail worn into the cliff-side – there was a 'drop' at the finish – I have no head for heights, so I closed my eyes, and leapt into John's outstretched embrace, cheered on by my fearless children, who would have been awaiting my arrival for some minutes. This route was a short cut to the beach, or so they said. I would have preferred to take the long, official route down.

Mostly, we had the beach to ourselves until mid-morning. The sea rushed in round rocks, boys and dog were dripping wet most of the time and once Billow swam out to sea after a beach ball, despite our cries of, 'Come back!' and when he was eclipsed by a roller, we thought he'd gone… The younger children were sobbing when the dog was spotted, staggering ashore, but wagging his sodden plume of a tail. He was soon wrapped in one of the family towels and I'm sure he was smiling in doggy fashion at all the cuddles and tidbits.

It was here that we had our first sight of Concorde. Amazing! Experimental flights were taking place around the coast. We shaded our eyes and craned our necks to watch this beautiful plane flying overhead.

At midday, more families came down to the beach. By then, the sun was beating down on us, and we had covered up bare limbs and retreated to the cool mouth of a cave at the foot of the cliffs. It worried me to see young parents carrying naked babies and toddlers without sun hats or tee shirts, running across sand which scorched bare feet. They believed their children were cooler without clothes, but they risked being terribly sunburnt.

We watched a wonderful display of kites one blowy day – the sky aerobatics were amazing. We acquired a box kite ourselves and had a great deal of fun. Sara, over the years, has made many unusual kites inspired by those days.

Another abiding memory is of the time Sara had a friend from Kent staying for a few days. We had been unable to park as usual by the cliff path down to the beach, and while we descended, John drove the minibus further up the road, and then joined us. When it was time to go home, he decided to scale the cliff beyond which the vehicle was parked. 'You go up the way we came down and I'll be there to pick you up, to save you the long hot trek up the road,' he promised.

We looked back as we made our way across the beach, to see him disappearing among a profusion of bushes higher up the cliff – he really would beat us to it, we thought!

We stood at the top, waiting, and waiting... Half an hour went by, then he had been gone more than an hour. We were becoming distinctly uneasy. Some people appeared at our level. I asked anxiously, 'Have you seen a tall man in shorts, walking along the beach?'

Heads were shaken. 'No. Most visitors went off the beach the other way... No-one down there, now.'

'He ... he went up the cliff, through the scrub – ages ago,' I said.

'Oh, it's like a jungle there – he'd never make it. Probably trying to get back.' Sympathetic smiles. 'He'll be back soon.'

But he wasn't. We could see the van in the distance, but we daren't leave where we were. Jonathan wasn't with us this day, he could have gone for help, I thought. The boys pleaded to go down on to the beach, promising no further, to see if they could spot their Dad.

It was almost dusk before the shout went up, 'Here he is!' and John, scratched and bleeding, shirt ripped, came wearily along the beach.

I'm not sure how the poor chap managed to drive home – we caught the last ferry – but the outcome could have been so much worse…

Seven

Good Old Bachelor Boys

Many families appeared to have an unmarried brother living with them. Some of these were solemn, quiet men who went to chapel and played bowls. They contrasted with their married brothers or brothers-in-law in that respect, who spent evenings in the pub with the parson. Often, it was the case that the bachelor brother, either the eldest or youngest of a big family, had looked after elderly parents before inheriting a run-down farm, or cottage, and then offered a married sister and her family, accommodation in return for keeping house.

We rarely saw these bachelors except when they came in for pipe tobacco. They appeared content with their lot.

There were two good old bachelor boys who lived together in a tiny whitewashed house, one up, one down, with no kitchen, just a gas ring in the hearth and a kettle suspended over a fire, no indoor sanitation (though this was common to the Cotts) a well in the back yard and a privy surrounded by nettles.

Fred, the elder brother, had been at sea most of his life – as a steward, not a sailor, he said. He was clean-shaven and his face had a ruddy glow. His brother Ted, with his stubbled chin and pale complexion, had been a bandsman in the army, been injured in the last war, and not able to work since. Fred was always dressed in a dark, pinstriped suit, collar and tie, plus a well-brushed bowler hat, when the brothers went to the pub. Ted, in old trousers held up by sagging braces, a shirt with frayed collar and cuffs, his wispy bald head uncovered, shuffled behind Fred and smiled his sweet, vague, toothless smile. They spent most of Saturday in the pub and then wove their unsteady way home via the shop.

Fred did all the talking. People said he fancied himself as a gentleman. Well, that is how we found him. In his cups yes, but polite and caring for his frail brother as best he could.

Fred produced a neatly written list. It never varied.

Half a pound of best Cornish butter.
A pint of milk.
A crusty small loaf.
Two tins of oxtail soup.
Two tins of garden peas.
Quarter of a pound of ham.
Small piece of strong cheddar.
Packet of Typhoo tea.
Sugar lumps.

Basket filled, he asked Ted if there was anything he wanted. Ted nodded. I handed him his weekly packet of cigarettes.

He spoke at last: 'Thank you madam.' Then they went home and it was easy to guess what they had for supper.

Red Crump was a stonemason and Mrs Trew's brother. There was no sign of it now, but we presumed he'd once had auburn hair like his sister. We had been living in the village for some months before we met him. He usually worked on projects away from his home, a chalet built on the Trew's land.

In our sitting room was a splendid stone fireplace, with two round granite knobs protruding on either side of the grate. We imagined that if you pressed or turned these protrusions, the whole fireplace might swing open (like fake bookcases in many a mystery movie) and reveal a hidden chamber behind. We didn't try to find out because those of us over the age of ten were aware it would spoil the illusion... The fascia was patterned with different shapes and colours – black, silver, white and even pink rocks.

One winter evening there was a knock on the front door. Mr Crump introduced himself, and a companion. 'May we come in? I wish to show him the fireplace I installed here, a few years ago.'

Why do visitors arrive when a room is untidy, I thought: I should have swept the hearth and polished the knobs... The only thing I could do was to persuade Billow to remove his sprawling body from the mat in front of the fire. The family escaped stealthily one by one to the kitchen, though Katy returned briefly to ask, 'Would Mr *Crumpet* like a cup of tea?' She had been put up to this by a larger sibling, judging by smothered giggles in the background.

He was seemingly too busy extolling the wonders of his work to notice this interruption.

The two men sat down on the sofa to discuss a price. I hovered helplessly and suppressed a gasp, when a large sum was agreed.

At last they turned to me, and Mr Crump said: 'Now, I think we can have that cup of tea!'

'Mum, you should have asked for a commission!' the children said.

Well, at least we inherited the fireplace, not paid for it, I thought.

Always without prior notification, Mr Crump called in from time to time to show off his masterpiece and to deliver his sales talk. But I told the family not to offer him and his clients any more cups of tea!

A single man moved into the cotts next door to the 'refugees' – I believe they were Polish and had arrived during the war. Mrs Slooski – the name sounded like that, but I never knew for sure – spoke broken English and always wore a headscarf. They didn't patronise the shop. Their new neighbour, a small man with impeccable manners, was a good customer, right from his first day in the village. We supposed him to be newly retired, certainly a bachelor, who enjoyed cooking for himself, and chatting pleasantly with John and me. We learned that he came from East Anglia, like my family, and he still had the burr.

'Even though I haven't been back there in years!' he remarked, when I said it was nice to be reminded of my Suffolk roots.

He was obviously a well-educated man, and we discussed books we had chosen in the library. He liked ancient history and bird books, like John.

A year or two later, it came as a shock to us to be told that our elderly friend was on parole from prison. He had been placed in our community by social workers.

'Whatever was someone like him doing in prison?' we wondered. He was affable and unassuming, patently honest, we thought. We were enlightened, 'He killed his wife twenty years ago.'

A few days on from this revelation, Mrs Slooski actually came into the shop to say, 'That man next door, he's gone away.' We never saw him again. We worried if he was all right. Would he be forced to keep 'moving on' when his past was revealed?

Eight

Platform Shoes and Lightning Strikes

Three daughters, two in their teens, accompanied their mother to help with weekend shopping. The older girls had jobs, and obviously enjoyed spending their wages on the latest fashions. They spoiled the youngest sister, Sharon and she too, tottered around on the highest platform shoes I have ever seen. On Saturdays they allowed her to delve into their makeup bags, and Sharon fluttered lashes thick with mascara and outlined her eyes with kohl. She was ten years old, with hefty limbs, not enhanced by brief emerald-green hot pants.

'I fell off me shoes,' she confided cheerfully to me one day.

'I'm not surprised!' I grinned back.

'Sprained me ankle,' Sharon added. She displayed a bandage.

'I see you know your right foot from your left, unlike Toddy!'

We'd spotted Toddy limping dramatically down the hill on a school day – by the time he reached the shop, John observed, 'He's limping on the other foot now!'

Toddy's explanation was that he had fallen down a rabbit hole, not as original as falling off your shoe.

There was a distinct rumble of thunder. Then a flash of lightning. The three Cox daughters gasped, grabbed at their mother.

'Now, now girls,' she said firmly. 'If you've seen it, it ain't struck you. But let's get the shopping done before it rains...' Despite these words, she was obviously in no hurry, for she had a story to tell me.

'My Sharon,' she said proudly, 'has been struck by lightning *three* times! She attracts it, you see.'

'Oh dear,' I said faintly, as the sky outside lit up once more. I added belatedly, 'Was she hurt?'

'Scorched,' Mrs Cox told me. 'Singed her hair, that's all.'

'Can't remember a thing about it,' Sharon was becoming bored.

It was raining by the time they left the shop. I worried whether Sharon would skid on the wet path and fall off her shoes again. And I crossed my fingers the lightning wouldn't find her attractive today.

Talking of shoes, there was a minor theft from the garage up the hill. A can of oil was missing and a few tools. The local bobby found a footprint in the mud. Later that day, Toddy visited the crime scene. To the garage owner's surprise, he removed his ancient trainer and fitted it to the impression.

His artless verdict was: 'Same pattern on the sole, same size as mine. Tell the bobby I reckon it's a size seven.'

I think he was actually disappointed not to be interviewed, following his detective work.

Our three boys were up on the moor and

caught in a thunderstorm one day. They were discovered sheltering in a hollow by a gang of the village boys who ambushed them and chased them, intent on having a scrap. One or two of these boys they had regarded as friends at school, but these had led the gang to them.

'Run home!' Chris shouted to his brothers. He was captured, bowled over and engulfed in a ruck.

He told us later, when we anointed his grazes and bruises, 'They were so busy thumping each other, I crawled out from under them and guess who helped me get away?'

We couldn't guess, we were still shocked to think they'd been set upon like that, with no provocation. Later, we would realise this was a rite of passage for newcomers.

'Wim,' he said. 'He appeared suddenly, he was by himself, and he grabbed hold of me, because I was on the edge where the land drops away, and we rolled all the way down to the bottom, that's where I got all the bumps and scratches, and the gang looked over and shouted, but didn't follow.'

Wim, that gentle giant of a boy was never involved in fights. We were glad our lads had a friend like him.

That first summer, storms were frequent. The sky would be blue, the sun blazed down then the rumbles began. One Wednesday afternoon, I went with John to the wholesalers. The two dogs were in the barn, with access to the enclosed back garden, but unable, we believed, to get out to the road side of the garden because we had secured the other door. We took these precautions because although the five-barred gate was a stout barrier, Florence could slide under it while Billow could jump it with ease.

The storm broke on our way home. Somehow, Billow barged the barn door open and the dogs took flight. They were missing for hours. Florence returned first, shivering and scared. We waited up, but no Billow. Some time during a wakeful night, we heard a bark. He was back! Ever after, he was terrified whenever he heard thunder, and needed reassurance. We never knew where they'd been that day.

Nine

What Can You Do With a Gallon of Ice-cream?

We learned along the village grapevine that the Hunt would be meeting outside the Crossroads Stores on Sunday morning.

'You'll be expected to open the shop,' we were told. 'The old owners reckoned it was well worth their while to do so.'

What could we tempt them with, we wondered. The sausage man came up with the answer. 'Ice-cream cornets!' He provided a gallon of his special recipe (family secret, of course), John got in the cornets and a scoop. I practised with mashed potato for a few days in advance.

Ginge painted a mouth-watering poster with a huge cornet overloaded with ice-cream and a chocolate flake bar for good measure.

The younger children sat on the front wall to await the arrival of the horses and the hunting fraternity. A crowd gathered opposite, by the stream. We turned the shop sign to OPEN. The girls peeked out through the front window.

Time went slowly until the allotted hour, nine o'clock. We had one customer before then, for a half-pound of sausages. I'd promised our lot a roast dinner later to celebrate selling all that ice-cream.

There was no chance now that any other of the locals could slip through. The forecourt was full of a moving mass of snorting horses and youngsters in smart jodhpurs, shiny boots and riding hats, using the mounting block to climb aboard a broad back. Most of them had riding crops which they used when their ponies fidgeted. Then suddenly the road was full of eager, panting hounds. The crowd moved back.

We'd become accustomed to soft clotted-cream voices with the expressions, 'good as gold', 'all right, my lover?' of those who came in the shop – the loud cut-glass accents of the men in pink and their ladies was unattractive; their arrogance, the way they ignored the local children who wanted to pet the horses was unkind. We were totally disregarded, too, hemmed in the shop, unable to open the door.

Before they cantered off, the hip flasks came out. We had not sold a single ice-cream. We consoled ourselves with a cornet apiece, then locked up, and decided ruefully to go out for the day as usual.

'Not to the moor,' the girls warned. 'Hope the fox gets away!'

In the middle of the night, John said aloud, 'What on earth can we do with a gallon of ice-cream?'

We thought we had the answer when there was news of a charity cycle ride. Our village was one of the stopping off points. The poster went up again, bunting decorated the village. But alas, the organisers failed to advise the parish council of a diversion. No cheers, no waves, no ice-cream…

We did get the order for selling cornets at the Vicarage Garden Fete, but naturally, that was our contribution, so all the special price ice-creams swelled the church roof fund.

There was still half a container of the stuff, yellower and stickier and harder to gouge out, but still edible, when the parson organised a community walk. John, Billow and the boys took part. It was eleven miles, and it was anticipated that the walk should take around 3 hours.

Katy, Maff and I were on ice-cream duty. The girls went off to the riding school. There weren't likely to be many other customers, after all.

The young ones were on look-out, perched as usual on the wall which separated shop from house. After about an hour, they came running in to report: 'Mummy, they're here!'

'They can't be,' I said, adding, 'Who?'

'Roger – and Wim!'

I could hardly believe my eyes, loping along came Wim in his worn plimsolls, with long dark hair flopping in his eyes, and just behind was our flaxen haired eleven year old Roger, who only came up to the big boy's shoulder. They were all smiles, and hardly out of breath.

'Where's Dad – Mike and Chris?' was all I could think of to say.

'Oh, they're *walking,*' Rog said. 'But we wanted to get back first for the ice-cream!'

So that's how we discovered Roger had a talent for long-distance running, and both he and Wim had a double flake in their cornets.

I still use the ice-cream scoop – for mashed potato.

We had visitors of our own all summer, but there were also the tourists, called grockels by the locals, who enquired: 'D'you know where we can get a cup of tea and a snack?'

I'm not sure who had the bright idea of a couple of small tables in the back garden and canvas chairs. The girls and I baked scones and flapjack (the boys' favourite, so we had to make extra for them) and fruit cake. All these went on the first Saturday afternoon, so then it had to be tea and biscuits, for 10p. The tourists lingered too long and we got hot and bothered, running to and fro from shop to garden. It was a short-lived experiment!

'We're a village shop and should stick to what people want,' John said. 'Not try all these other things.'

Well, we did know what they wanted. Jumbo pink sausages…

Ten

Maff and the Big Bar of Chocolate

Maff was our junior assistant in the year before he joined his sister at school. He only 'worked' part-time of course, when he felt like it. He was a favourite with all our female customers, pointing out the day's bargains and locating other items for them. They patted his curly head and advised: 'Don't cut his hair yet, will you?' I was aware that John, who believed boys should look like boys, was hoping to wield the scissors one day when I wasn't looking... Anyway, I knew he couldn't go to school with that mop of ringlets. 'He'll tell us when he wants to be shorn,' I said feebly, and in my defence trotted out the old story of a mother we knew who worried her child wouldn't be parted from her dummy – this little girl went to the dustbin the evening before she started at school, lifted the lid, and dropped the mangled comforter inside. '*She* decided for herself,' I said.

(Maybe this is the time to confess, that like John's kipper tie, somewhere I have secreted away an envelope with guess-what inside…)

Once a week, a dear old chap came into the shop, half an hour before the bus to town was due. He was always dressed up with a Fair Isle pullover under a thick, hairy sports jacket, however hot the weather. Like Fred and Ted, he invariably bought the same goods as he had the previous week.

'I'm off to see my daughter,' he explained the first time we met. 'I like to contribute towards our lunch.'

John sliced three-quarters of a pound of best ham and I weighed out tomatoes, selected a curly lettuce, and popped four rolls in a bag.

If Maff was in the garden, he would twitch his nose, scenting the smell of Mr Brightling's Three Nuns tobacco, even though he always removed and tapped his pipe on the wall before entering the shop.

'Here comes the boy,' Mr B beamed. 'Now, while you tot that lot up my dear – don't forget the tobacco, will you? My allowance for the week! I'll let my young friend choose something *he* fancies, eh?'

He led his young friend by the hand to the chocolate display. Maff considered the Milky Ways. Mr B reached his long arm over the counter and selected a half-pound bar of fruit and nut. 'That's more like it, isn't it?'

By then I had rung up the till and packed Mr B's shopping in his bag. I had already passed over the tobacco and his change.

'Thank you kindly, goodbye.' And Mr B was gone. I could never bring myself to remind him that he hadn't paid for Maff's treat – I held out my hand to Maff and said: 'I don't think you'd enjoy that, darling. How about…' I indicated the threepenny candy. He was happy with six fruit chews and I was able to replace the expensive big choc bar.

Phew! I thought. One of these days he'll open the wrapper before I can retrieve it ... then I won't have the heart to take it away.

It's known as 'eating the profits', you see.

John's mother and two sisters arranged to stay not far from us our second summer and over the Bank Holiday, we had a lovely weekend with them, seeing the sights, and spending a day at our favourite estuary beach. Grandma Lottie, whom we all adored, seemed not quite herself, and a few months later was diagnosed with a serious illness. It was then that we realised how far away we were from our families. My father, eighteen years older than my mother, had recently celebrated his eightieth birthday, but now, he too was ill, after suffering a stroke.

'You must go and see them,' John thought, concerned. 'As they can't come to visit us.' Both families had been so generous and encouraging in their support for our life-changing move. Now they needed us, we were not on hand to help.

'Oh, I can't leave you with the shop and the family – it's too much,' I replied.

'You could take Katy with you. Ginge and the boys are off school, Jo has a break from college, they'll keep an eye on Maff, so, of course you can!' John said firmly.

I capitulated gracefully. Best to go while most of the older children were still at home, I realised. Sara was working at the television studios and had recently appeared on local TV in an amazing patchwork dress she had designed and made herself. She was planning to study fine art in Wimbledon, after a foundation year, also away from home. JP had passed his driving test, he had decided to look further afield with regard to work... Anyway, I was only going away for a few days.

Katy and I travelled by train. We were met in London by John's sister, who kindly drove us home to my parents in Surrey.

I was kept entertained throughout the long journey by my lively little daughter. We sat in the buffet car, and she soon spread her comics out on the table and read and chattered at the same time.

In the seat opposite was a stern-looking woman who ignored us and turned the pages of a paper-back.

It was a beautiful day, and the coastal route was breath-taking at times. Sparkling water, golden sands, under a cloudless sky. I felt myself relaxing. I must have dozed at one point, because I awoke with a start to hear Katy say, as she leaned on her elbows and regarded our fellow passenger, 'Can you take your teeth out, like my granddad?'

'Certainly not,' was the sharp reply, the first words the woman had spoken in more than two hours.

Even as I opened my mouth to apologise, Katy, not put off by our fellow passenger's abruptness, decided to enlarge on what she'd said before. 'My granddad can do tricks with his teeth. He can make them shoot out, and then go back, with his tongue. I can whistle, because my two front teeth dropped out.

Can you whistle?'

'I ... it's impolite to whistle.'

'We have to whistle our dog. Shall I show you how I do it?'

'No thank you.' But there was a little twitch at the corners of the woman's mouth. She glanced at me. 'You are very fortunate to have such a bright child,' she said unexpectedly.

'Thank you...'

While we had lunch, and Katy made a noise sucking lemonade through a straw, I thought, now I have a story to make dear Oz smile. When I was Katy's age, I had nicknamed my dad Oz, because his second name was Osmund. In return he called me Shelag, when I decided (for a week or two!) to change the spelling of my name to Sheelagh. I thought that was how it was pronounced!

It made my mum smile too, which was good, after all the worry she'd been through recently. 'We've missed you,' she said, hugging us.

John and Maff met us at the station when we returned. The first thing I saw was a little boy with cropped hair. No longer a baby. It's a fact of life, as my mum once pointed out to me, that babies grow up, just as puppies and kittens do... You have to accept it.

'He was so hot and sticky, with all that hair, it was the kindest thing,' John said in his defence. 'Ginge did it – I thought I might bodge it! We trimmed Billow first, for the same reason...'

There was a lump in my throat. I knew he was right. 'Did you use the same scissors?' I asked huskily.

Eleven

Sunken Sugar

After the glorious summer, down came the rain. It was an autumn of coughs and sneezes. John and I were on the receiving end of all the germs and bugs going round the village, in the shop. We sold a lot of patent remedies and sympathised with our customers. We listened patiently to the tales of woe and no-one noticed that we also had watery eyes and red noses, or realised that we had sick, querulous children calling for our attention, too.

I suppose we should have seen disaster coming. After all, we had always had to keep an eye on river levels near our old home, although water never encroached our property in our time there, even if we were marooned because the road was flooded.

The babbling brook opposite the shop was lashed into a torrent by hours of relentless rain. Even the ducks flew away. Customers waded through puddles to buy tobacco, but not much else. Even the sausages stayed in the freezer. Sales of paraffin were up.

We went to bed with hot water bottles, a box of tissues and aspirin. Early next morning, around 4 a.m., we were woken by a thunderous knocking on the front door. Struggling into our dressing gowns, and wondering who on earth it could be, we went downstairs. Mr Trew and two other men, in oilskins and thigh-high fishing boots, stood there.

'The road's flooded. Came to see you were all right…' Water lapped at the step. 'Check the shop,' Mr Trew advised. 'The floor's lower that end. Close the door. I'll bring you some sandbags a bit later.' They went off to see what they could do for the folk in the Cotts.

We stepped into ankle-deep water at the

front of the shop. We hadn't thought to change our slippers for wellington boots. We spotted some submerged objects, the contents of the bottom shelf of the main unit – bags of sugar. No pea-green boat, as the rhyme goes, and we'd lost more than a five-pound note... We captured the bloated packets and placed them in a nearby bucket.

The sugar, fortunately, was the only casualty of the flood, but we were mopping up for hours, still in our night attire and belatedly, rubber boots. Most of our neighbours were similarly occupied.

Later, John rescued the damp bundle of daily newspapers, and got on with the marking up. Fortunately, family had slept on through the dramatic events.

'Porridge for breakfast,' I decided. Seemed the simplest thing.

The flood outside slowly drained away. Mrs Trew came over to commiserate with us. 'Didn't the folk before you say about the flood they had just after they moved in? The water ruined the carpet in the living rooms.

They got enough back on the insurance to buy that lovely green carpet you've got in there now. Three hundred pounds it cost.'

I smiled wryly. 'They charged us an *extra five hundred* for that!'

Mind you, we took the carpet up when we left, and it lasted us a good twenty years. So I suppose we had our money's worth, eh?

The brook dried up during the drought of 1976. There was a hose pipe ban, a restriction on use of water generally. The reservoir a few miles away was empty, standpipes were installed in the villages. Life became very difficult for us all, especially the farming community.

The reality of living here was very different to the holidays we had enjoyed in the West Country in the past. Stories were related of other troubled times – folk here recalled the terrible winter of 1962-3, which was very like our own experience of being snowbound for months in rural Kent.

Mrs Diddley leaned over the counter to

tell me in a confidential whisper: 'There was a coal lorry, got stuck in a drift on the hill. It stayed there until it thawed.'

'Oh, dear,' I murmured faintly, almost overcome by the reek of bleach from her person.

'Then,' she said, as if she still couldn't believe it, 'they discovered that all the sacks of coal had gone… No-one knows who dug down through all that snow, to this day.'

When I repeated this tale to John later, he said simply: 'Didn't they check who had smoke coming out of their chimney?'

The local M.P. came into the shop one day, to enquire how we were coping. The locals crowded in behind him to air their grievances. He listened sympathetically, then apologised that he must go – other hamlets to call on.

'Shan't vote for him next time,' some said. 'Him in his grey suit and Tory blue tie.'

I don't imagine that most of them had the first time! Politicians were viewed with great suspicion. Only Lloyd George was mentioned with affection. 'He got us the old age pension,' they said. 'He's a good old boy.' I don't think they accepted he was no longer around.

The girls worried about the wild ponies on the moors. They were running short of food. There was an airlift of supplies to the ponies, and much publicity in the papers and on T.V. They also complained about sharing bath water. They didn't want to hear my oft repeated story about nine people taking turns in the old tin tub during the war, topped-up from a kettle of hot water and soap flakes to mask the scum. 'We know, Mum, you were number three, and you wondered what the baby had done in the water, before it was your turn,' they sighed.

'I didn't make a fuss like you are...'

'We had a bath that fitted under the kitchen table, when we lived in the country,' John put in. 'You lifted off the top and filled the tub from the copper where the sheets were boiled on Mondays…'

To the girls, that was beyond the pale.

We queued patiently at the standpipe, with a variety of containers. Toddy, of course, had Corona bottles. I hoped he would hang on to them because our supply of soft drinks was exhausted.

Every village received a consignment of bottled water. It didn't go far to solve the problem, but we were grateful.

The atmosphere was boiling, not simmering. When eventually it rained again, everyone rushed outside in great excitement and relief. There wasn't quite dancing in the street, but the crisis was coming to an end.

Twelve

Going Out

It came to us all of a sudden, the realisation that our daughters were no longer biddable small girls, but attractive young women. They were about to launch themselves on the world, and determined to make an impression. We were so proud of them and their achievements, but their new-found independence made us feel a little sad. Maybe, even, rather redundant…

Our small daughter and son helped to alleviate the sense of loss you inevitably feel when your grown up children dismiss the old and familiar. You don't know then that when the grandchildren come along, they'll bring them up with the same values as you did with them. That's a great feeling.

At the doctors one day, I was catching up on my reading in the waiting room, and settled Katy with a book too. She was in line for a booster injection. I was suddenly aware that the solemn people all around us were laughing. I looked up, and saw a smiling man with one foot, hopping across to the nearest available chair. How could they be insensitive enough to laugh at that, I thought. Then, to my embarrassment, I saw Katy, in her bright red jumper and kilt, hopping behind him.

'You won!' she told her new friend, as he sat down.

'Please don't apologise,' the man said to me. 'She made my day!'

Spring time, and a young man's fancy and all that: knocks on the front door in the evening meant the girls were going out, probably with one of the public school types from the select estate up the hill... A dashing chap in a sports car called for Jo. (Some years later she married him!) Sara had a boyfriend at that time who wore a cape and a homburg hat, but it wouldn't be too long before she was picking gherkins in Sweden, with the young man she would eventually marry. There was also a lovelorn local boy who presented me with flowers on my birthday, hoping to win *her* approval. I had endless teasing about that! Ginge tried to convince us there was safety in numbers, going out with a group of excitable girls and boys for rambles on the moors. It would be a few years yet before she met her soul-mate at teacher-training college.

(In due course, all three of them were happily married, Jo and Ginge two weeks apart and Sara a while later… Jonathan beat them all to it, when he was just 22! After two years, *we* were young grandparents!)

Ponies and riding on the moors might be no longer the girls' main interest, but the boys stuck to their football sessions, though they were developing a taste for pop bands. Maff was getting into football, but naturally he trailed behind them with regard to pop concerts! Though he did eventually inherit

Roger's *The Water Boys* teeshirt! I miss that on the washing line nowadays!

We bought a radiogram, and now there were tussles over choice of records. It was no longer just the weekly discos which kept us awake, we had our own disco going on downstairs at night, clashing with Martha's more uplifting music upstairs... Gilbert O'Sullivan lingers on in our record collection, but the Beatles records, which belonged to John, disappeared one by one.

I don't wish to dwell on teenage angst, suffice it to say that running a shop, with all its restrictions, is not the ideal situation with adolescents. Waiting up anxiously at nights, listening out for noisy car exhausts, means bleary eyes next day...

Christmas came round again, and now I didn't get hot round the collar when Mrs Deans' big girls, who appeared to share the care of the baby, now a toddler, who had arrived unexpectedly on our first Christmas Day in the shop, asked for 'crap paper.' I only twigged the first time when one added, 'You know, for decorations. Red and green crap paper…'

With relief, I bypassed the stack of Bronco rolls, and pointed out the crepe paper.

John strung coloured lights all round the shop and we enjoyed filling a few shelves with toys and items for the Christmas stockings. The previous Christmas we had sold out of seasonal gifts, and the mince pies, Dundee and Tunis cakes, chocolate logs and boxes of luxury chocs sold like, well, hot cakes.

'I gave Toddy's mother a lift down the hill,' John said ruefully. 'She was loaded down with all her shopping. I couldn't drive past when she was struggling, could I?'

We really couldn't condemn them for buying things in the new supermarket near the new estate.

We had the old faithfuls, thank goodness, but how long could we last out? Funds were low. Expenses high. We had to keep the shop well-stocked.

One of our favourite customers was unwell. A friend of Fred and Ted called into the shop one Saturday.

'Would you be kind enough to deliver their usual order, later on?'

Of course we would. We enquired tactfully as to what was wrong with Ted.

'Oh, it's not him as is ill – it's poor old Fred. A stroke, I reckon. They've never registered with the doctor. Ted can't look after him – my Missus is going to get in touch with their sister. Doris was a housekeeper in Somerset, but she's retired now. She's younger than them, and the cottage will be hers, when they go.'

I added a bunch of grapes, from us, to the order, and Ted's cigarettes.

Later, I rattled the letterbox, there was no knocker on the door.

There was the sound of shuffling feet, but it took Ted a while to open the door. He'd had difficulty in getting round the bed which took up most of the narrow passageway which led from the living room.

'Step inside,' he said. 'Say hello to Fred.' It was the most I'd ever heard him say.

In the gloom, I made out an inert form, covered with a grey army blanket. Fred's face was pale, his mouth a little awry. I saw then that, without the familiar bowler hat, he was as bald as Ted.

'Hello Fred,' I said, feeling that was inadequate. 'How are you?'

'He can't speak.' Ted leaned over his brother, extracted something from under his pillow. He held out Fred's purse to me, trusting me to take the right money for the groceries.

I could tell that Fred was struggling to say something, but he couldn't manage it. I touched the thin hands, motionless on the blanket.

'Thank you,' I managed. 'I hope you feel better soon…' I handed the carrier bags to Ted. 'Take care of him…' I thought, poor old Ted can't take care of himself…

As Ted saw me out he said, 'Don't worry.

Our Doris is coming tomorrow.'

'That's good,' I said. 'I'll call again soon.'

I told John later, 'I don't think we'll see poor old Fred again.' Sadly, Fred passed away the day after his sister arrived. Ted wasn't allowed out on his own. Doris came in the shop one day to tell us that she would be moving into the cottage permanently.

'I could have coped with dear Fred, but not Ted. He's never been all there, since he got wounded in the head in the war, you see. He was such a musical lad. Played the trombone. Anyway, there's only one bedroom, so he's going to a residential home up the hill. By the way, I was clearing out some of their rubbish, and I opened up a cupboard and a whole lot of tins fell out…' She looked at me suspiciously.

I could guess: oxtail soup, garden peas, I thought…

'I don't suppose you want to buy 'em all back? I'm a regular at the Co-op, always have been.'

I couldn't help hesitating, biting my lip.

'I suppose not,' Doris sighed. 'I know I wouldn't. Oh, if Ted should get down here and ask you for cigarettes, he's not to have them. Doctor's orders. *Don't forget!*' She departed.

We missed our good old bachelor boys.

Thirteen

The Little Shop Can Save Your Bacon

Our neighbour, Martha rushed into the shop in a panic one morning. 'The butcher's let me down! We've no meat for the school dinners today!' she exclaimed dramatically, at full throttle, rather as she had been last night when the organ music had swelled and she had sung *Lily of Laguna,* not once but three times, obviously practicing for an Olde Tyme concert, planned by Rev. Bouncy Ball.

'Ham?' John suggested helpfully.

'Hot meal today – what else can you suggest?'

'I've several big packs of bacon, Miss Dingle delivered the eggs yesterday – how about eggs, bacon and, sausages of course!'

'Chips?' I said. I thought, half-a-dozen of Les's huge spuds would be enough to feed the children. I knew Martha had a machine to slice 'em.

'A fry up! They'd love that,' Martha agreed. This was before school meals had to be low fat et al, no doubt Martha would use slabs of lard in the cooking. 'Will you pack all that up please and deliver it to the school as soon as possible? I must get on!'

I volunteered to make the delivery. I'd never been in the school kitchen, indeed, it occurred to me, as I hurried along to the school, that I had not been invited into any of the village homes, apart from Miss Dingle's once, when she wanted to show us her new colour T.V. It really was 'them and us,' we were tolerated by most, made use of, as now, but we didn't belong here, and probably never would. Like Rev. Bouncy Ball, who tried so hard to get things going in the village, we were outsiders. It came to me then, that we had made no close friends in the area. We were fortunate that we had old friends, John and Joyce in Launceston whom we'd known since school days, but due to the long hours we worked, we were unable to meet up often. The other John was kind enough to audit our accounts: he'd recently warned us that the Recession was adversely affecting small businesses. We'd taken on the Crossroads Stores at the wrong time…

Six people sat round the table in the School kitchen. It was ten-thirty, the children were in the playground, Katy and Maff, who had just joined her at school, waved to me as I went inside. In the centre of the table was the largest treacle tart I had ever seen, glistening golden and obviously just out of the oven. Martha was cutting slices of this, and passing them to her two assistants, the two dinner ladies, and – I thought I could smell bleach! – Mrs Diddley. One of the helpers was pouring tea from a big teapot. My tummy rumbled.

Martha waved a sticky hand in greeting. 'Could you put the bacon etc, in the fridge please? Send the bill into the school. You'll be paid at the end of the month. Thanks!' This was a blow. We'd hoped to be paid from the petty cash. John would need to buy more bacon now.

The treacle tart plate was empty. I wondered if the children would be as lucky. I wasn't offered a cup of tea. But I was glad for Elsie Diddley's sake that she was included in the gathering. I hoped her tart didn't taste of bleach!

As I returned to man the counter, tears pricked my eyes. I thought back to the days when I was 'just a mum' and made special things for the children's tea. I didn't get time for that now. I missed my dear friend Liz, who always put the kettle on when I called round at hers, just as I did, when she came to mine. I knew that John missed our old life, too. He missed going on sales trips, his colleagues at work.

All I said to John was, 'D'you know, I haven't written anything except letters since we've been here…'

The very next day he arrived back from the wholesalers with an advance birthday present for me – an Olivetti portable typewriter. I had it for years and most of the children's stories I wrote then, were tapped out on the kitchen table. It was just as easy to use as a laptop.

The parson called one day to ask if we would help with the annual Vicarage garden fete as usual. In a lull between customers, we offered him refreshment. We opened up to him about some of our misgivings about how long we might last out here, and in turn he told us that he was the only child of a widowed mother, that he'd been brought up in a flat above the family confectioners and tobacconists, in a grim, industrial area in the north of England. He'd won scholarships and gone to university.

After being a curate in an inner-city slum area, he'd been offered the job of parish priest here. He'd jumped at the chance, brought his mother with him, and his new wife.

'Things didn't turn out as I expected,' he said slowly. His round, cherubic face was flushed. He didn't enlarge on that, but I don't think he was just referring to village life.

His simple advice was to sell up before we lost all we had worked so hard for over the years.

So, you could say, that a treacle tart led to an advertisement in the same national newspaper where we'd learned of the availability of the Crossroads Stores, in 'idyllic West Country village'…

It was almost a year before we sold up, and we thought initially, we should stay around the area, because of the boys' schooling, as they were all due to take O levels within the next few years, and Ginge, A levels. The employment prospects were not very encouraging. Our older children would likely all soon be working, or studying, elsewhere. However, property was still available for much less, than in the south.

So in the interval between, we actually

enjoyed looking over suitable, and often not so suitable! places on our Sundays off. One that I recall, was not far from the edge of a cliff. Some of the garden had gone over. The cellar that ran the length of the house, was fitted up as a games room. The boys, naturally, were enthusiastic about that! Another property was built into a hillside, with a moss roof. This was a nature reserve (in miniature) where a local Naturalist and his wife, with wild hair had lived in a state of chaos for many years. They wore kaftans and beads and had filthy, hardened bare feet. We didn't get any further than the jungle of a garden – we weren't prepared to hack our way through the giant nettles. Katy and Maff couldn't stop giggling.

We didn't see many prospective buyers for the shop, either. We became resigned to the fact that we would be there a while yet…

Fourteen

Then the Wall Fell Down

The growing Recession was hitting us hard. Despite all our continuing efforts to make a go of things, it was a case of keeping our heads above water. To quote another metaphor, most of our customers were in the same boat – we were all struggling.

We had two farmers to whom we delivered weekly. The first was a wealthy gentleman farmer, the second was a tenant farmer. Both put in a large order on a Friday and John delivered a box full of groceries on Saturday afternoon. We were paid promptly, and this contribution to our income was vital.

I was away, visiting our families, we did this in turn, when the first farmer failed to put his order in as usual. John, extra busy, was actually relieved not to have to pack and deliver these goods. We fully expected to see this farmer the following week, but again, no list appeared. Then John, at the wholesalers one day, spotted our gentleman farmer wheeling a trolley. He had obtained a card, and he was not the only one. We just wished he could have told us, and not left us to find out. We couldn't blame him for getting his goods at cost price, now times were difficult.

Farmer no. 2 continued to buy from us, but he couldn't always pay on time. We received half a lamb in part-payment, then a small turkey, and finally, he, too had a card and took his custom elsewhere.

Wim's mother, another of the small parents of large offspring, came in the shop every day. She could never make her mind up. She lingered by the freezer for about half an hour, trying to decide what to buy. I stood by patiently, making the occasional suggestion. The outcome was predictable.

Her worried expression would clear, a decision had been made. It was always the same: 'Six sausages, please. You can't go wrong with sausages, can you?'

Six sausages among four people, I thought. Wim could probably eat that many by himself. I never knew whether she was a single parent on a very restricted income, or if she had a husband who was unemployed. She was one of a minority who did things the old way: she paid once a week, and her daily purchases were marked in a dog-eared little book, with a pencil attached by string. Recently, she had paid a week in arrears, and it was becoming obvious that she was unable to catch up. This was preferable to the less reliable customers who promised to pay 'in a day or two', but never came near the shop again. We were forced to take one of these unscrupulous people (not a local) to the small claims court, but never received a penny, because 'he had no assets.'

Mrs Diddley's sister called in regularly, but didn't actually purchase anything. 'Just looking,' she said. Unlike her sister, she was obviously a lady of leisure, well-dressed, with no children and a husband who worked. She had a perpetually mournful expression, though she enjoyed relating details of her latest operation – 'They opened me up to remove a *sponge* they left inside last time,' she said, awaiting my reaction. I rose to the challenge. 'How awful – how did that happen?' I shouldn't have asked. John always disappeared when he saw her coming, saying she was a time-waster. Ever hopeful, I thought she might buy a little something on our very last day – she didn't.

The strain was beginning to tell. I had suffered from psoriasis in my teens and now it returned with a vengeance. I was allergic to the ointments then prescribed – my only consolation was that the worst patches were on my legs, not my face – though I felt a pariah on the beach.

We learned from Mrs Trew that there were rumours going around that we were selling up.

'It doesn't seem likely,' I said truthfully, 'right now.'

She patted my shoulder. 'You're missing home, my dear. We'll be sorry if you go, but you must do what's best for you and the family.' I took that to mean I had her blessing.

When I repeated this conversation to John and the older children, Ginge said: 'She's right. We should go back to Kent. We fitted in there.'

'But ... what about your schooling – you, in particular?' we queried. In September she would be in her final A level year, and was doing exceptionally well.

'I'll cope,' she assured us. 'Sara will be in Wimbledon by then, and Jo will be glad to leave her job anyway – her boss is always going on about his double hernia!' Jo did a 'wicked' impression of this man, who made his female staff blanch, when he opened a box delivered to the office and proudly displayed the contents – a formidable truss – to the startled young ladies.

'If a buyer turns up soon for the shop,

we'll definitely think about it,' John and I agreed.

The boys were excited at the prospect of being again within reach of Chelsea and Arsenal football grounds, and Katy and Maff were, we felt, still young enough to adapt to a move. JP was also working temporarily in London with his uncle. We'd see more of him, which would be great.

If only we could return to Crabapple Cottage, we thought, but we knew that wasn't possible…

We advertised the shop one more time – we had to lower the price. The post office pair had already departed without selling: this might help us we thought, if a buyer for the stores bid for the post office franchise.

We knew we would have to start 'all over again,' look for a property in need of modernising, as the cottage had been. It wouldn't be easy for John to find a job, either, now he was over forty, in the economic crisis.

A couple in their fifties, with a nest-egg,

came to view. They drove a hard bargain, but they were cash buyers. We weren't in a position to turn them down, but we wanted a little time to consider their offer.

The deciding moment came when the garden wall fell down.

John and I were in the kitchen, rustling up our lunch. We were on our own as we always were Monday to Friday. It was a lovely day. I looked out of the window. Should we eat outside at the millstone table and soak up the sunshine, I wondered. Then, I couldn't believe my eyes – 'John!' I yelled. 'Look what's happening!'

The dry-stone wall which marked our property was tumbling, in slow motion, stone by stone, with a domino effect, in a cloud of dust. There was a faint rumble, like distant thunder. Billow, fortunately he was indoors enjoying his meat and biscuits, lifted his head and howled.

We were both speechless for a minute or two, trying to comprehend what was happening.

‘Thank goodness,’ John said at last, ‘it didn’t happen when the children were playing out there…’

There was now a big gap in the wall, and rubble strewn over the path. We were expecting the prospective buyers to return in three days for our answer – repairs were vital. We sought the advice of Mr Trew. The wall, he thought had been built a century ago. Each stone would have to be painstakingly returned to its original place. It was like a jigsaw puzzle. No lunch for us – it took John two days to build back the wall.

We’d come to a decision though. We’d cut our losses and sell.

This was not the final disaster, but then, as the saying goes, things always happen in threes.

Our buyers were not ready to move by the time school began in September. The girls went to stay with relatives in Kent, after helping John decide on the location of our new home. Jo, with excellent secretarial skills, soon found temporary work – Ginge went to an All-Girls (she didn't like that bit!) Grammar School in Maidstone. The young ones continued at the village primary school, but I was advised it would cause less upheaval for the three boys if we tutored them at home for a couple of weeks. They were given set work. They had places lined up at a good school in Kent.

As I was busy in the shop, I had to trust they would concentrate on their studies... One day when I wasn't able to supervise properly, they decided to be helpful and bring down some items from the loft. This they did, but they kept quiet about the fact that running along the rafters, one of them had slipped and his foot had gone through our bedroom ceiling... Knowing I wouldn't get a chance to go upstairs until that evening, they hatched a make do and mend solution.

Gullible Mum allowed them out for a breath of fresh air that afternoon. I was unaware that they had pooled their pocket money and bought a can of white paint, lining paper and wallpaper paste. Michael, our mathematical wizard, worked out what they could afford. The ceiling was duly patched, hopefully by him as he had the most practical skills, while I was still occupied in the shop!

I am now going to quote from a composition which Katy later wrote at her new school, after the move – this incident obviously made a lasting impression on her after the consequence was discovered.

One day, my mum and dad were lying in bed, and my Dad looked up at the ceiling. 'My God, Sheila,' he cried 'What's that?' Mum looked up. 'What do you mean?' she asked. Dad shouted, 'Can't you see it? That patch on the ceiling. It was not there when I went away, don't you ever look up?' 'I'm too busy looking down,' Mum said. Dad went to find out what it was and he nearly fell through too. He said 'how can we sell this place now?' But we did.

Katy's teacher had given this 8 out of 10,

with the comment, 'What an interesting story.'

The third thing happened on moving day, after the contract was signed and the contents etc. agreed. The big kitchen fridge conked out, we had to call out an engineer and to pay the bill there and then.

Fifteen

Goodbye

Our last weeks in the Crossroads Stores were surprisingly busy ones. Most of the village came in to say they were sorry we were going, and to wish us well. It was heartwarming. I was even invited on a Chapel outing to the beach, with Katy and Maff, and for the first time I felt among friends, but it was too late...

There were gifts from the regular customers, including tea towels from Mrs Diddley and chocolates from devotees of the Co-op.

Those who filled the shelves, whether they were due to call or not, came loaded with their specialities and hoped we would recommend them to the new owners.

Tinkerbelle gave me a pair of sheer tights. Not the most tactful present with my bad leg. 'Lissel' would have been more of a cover-up.

During the final week, John had to travel up to Kent to tie up loose ends there – the girls were the only other members of the family to view our new abode, all I knew was that it was a 'partly converted Methodist chapel.' It was all we could afford with sufficient accommodation, though (as I was about to discover when we arrived there) no interior doors and a temporary staircase, more a ladder, leading to the gallery, unprotected by a rail…

While John was away, a familiar figure appeared in the shop. The bus had stopped at the Crossroads, and would wait there ten minutes or so, before turning back up the hill. It was midday, and a single passenger disembarked.

I wasn't too sure if I was seeing things. Ted, in pyjamas, dressing gown and slippers, smiled his sweet smile. He had obviously dodged the carers at the Home, and slipped out.

Then I focused on the unfortunate fact that Ted had not 'adjusted his frontispiece', that his trousers were gaping – but how could I tell him that?

'It's good to see you, Ted,' I managed.

He pointed, with a trembling finger at the cigarette shelf. His breathing was laboured, and I remembered his sister Doris's strictures. I also recalled that Mrs Diddley had told me Doris was away.

'Oh, Ted, I'm so sorry,' I said, 'but you're not allowed to smoke, are you? Does anyone know you've come down here? I think you ought to catch the bus back…'

I came round the counter and took his arm. 'Come on, old boy.'

The bus driver hastily put out his cigarette, jumped down to help Ted aboard. 'He didn't have any money on him for the fare – but I couldn't turn him off, could I? I waited, guessed you'd suggest he make the return journey. I'll see him inside the

Home, don't worry.'

'Goodbye, Ted.' I was choked, because it really *was* goodbye.

(Remembering Ted (and Fred, of course) while writing this, I realise he must be long gone … I like to think he plays his trombone again in Heaven.)

On Thursday evening, John and I checked the stock for the last time. It was past 1 a.m. when we finally staggered to bed, exhausted. It was a comfort to know that Joyce and John were coming to help us load up the container lorry from Kent. We got that at a special rate because it had brought a load down here, and would have returned empty to base. It would even be possible to transport the small boat John had recently acquired, for 'a song' but never had time to use. (In fact, it was so decrepit, the cat took it over as his quarters!)

Before first light, I was roused by the sound of a heavy vehicle grinding to a halt, opposite the shop, beside the stream. There were voices, lights came on, then were switched off.

John looked at his watch. It was 4 a.m. The new owners, who had also hired a large lorry, were here. They had travelled by night, just as we had done three and a half years ago. But they weren't due to arrive until 10 a.m.

'They're obviously settling down for the rest of the night – so we should too,' John said wisely, guessing that I was about to get up, to boil the kettle, and to take them cups of tea.

We rose at 5.30 as usual, but stripped the bed and rolled the bedding – one job done, we thought. Fortunately the three girls had packed their belongings before they left, after sorting out what they could take with them. Their beds were already dismantled.

There are always things you can't do until you are about to move out. John opened the front door cautiously to retrieve the papers, but there was no sign of anyone stirring over the road.

The boys started on their allotted jobs – their cases were already packed. At 8, kind Mrs Trew came over to take Katy and Matthew over to her house and to give them breakfast.

'Anne has planned some games to keep them occupied,' she said. We were very grateful.

The boys cooked a greasy plateful apiece of sausages, eggs and beans. John and I opted for boiled eggs and toast. Then I went into the shop to carry on until the new owners officially took over, while John mustered his troops and awaited the arrival of our helpers. They didn't let us down, arriving within half an hour.

Everything sold before 10 a.m. had to be jotted down in a notebook. The removal team had cleared the upstairs by then, but the dining room was chock-a-block with boxes awaiting their attention. Things were going according to plan it seemed, until the newcomers began moving their stuff inside... This was an hour before we'd agreed they could, but they were obviously eager to take over.

At this point, a couple of unmarked boxes (which we didn't discover until they were opened up a few days later) made their way onto our vehicle. We gained a couple of blankets but the incomers did rather better with a chest of drawers!

Mrs Cooper was eager to take my place behind the counter. However, I couldn't do much to help the workers out back (where the container lorry was parked) as every few minutes I was called upon to explain something to her. She reported excitedly on her first customer – 'Well, he didn't actually buy anything, but he introduced himself, Toddy, I think he said his name was. He had six bottles to return, and he told me how much the deposit was, and when I paid him (lucky you'd put some cash in the till) he said thank you very politely. What a nice boy!'

I couldn't disillusion her so soon. 'I should bring the crate inside,' I said, 'for today, in case someone trips over it, with all the coming and going.' As I thought, the crate was empty, the six bottles it had contained were now lined up on the counter.

I don't know why, but my gaze was drawn to the perfume bottles by the mirror. I suppressed a groan. Two were missing! The stock list would have to be adjusted.

Then I made all the workers large mugs of strong, sugared tea, to keep their strength up.

It was well past lunch-time when the two Johns began their final task, rolling up the thick-piled green carpet and then the rubber underlay. Joyce and I followed them with a broom apiece to sweep the floor.

'We must go,' they said. They had boys of their own at home.

We said goodbye and thank you to our wonderful friends, and knew we would miss them, but thank goodness the bond between us has endured, and I know it always will be strong.

The lorry drove off. We hoped to be

reunited with our goods and chattels the following morning in Kent.

Now, we had our personal possessions and the overflow (which included the pets!) to pack into the minibus – by late afternoon we were on our way, hoping to arrive in the wee small hours at our Chapel.

Sixteen

A Moving Experience

The mini-bus was packed to the gunwales. Due to that darn boat, we'd had to accommodate some pieces of furniture in the back. (I couldn't be a Jonah and tell John off, could I, when he'd been working flat out? Anyway, what about all my writing paraphernalia?) This meant the boys, dog, cat, tortoises and goldfish (Maff's) were hemmed in. We assured them we'd stop off for fish and chips and then they could snooze while Dad drove on as far as he could before the next break... We even optimistically thought we might arrive at the chapel by midnight. As none of the girls or JP were with us, we felt incomplete after so many family outings. I had the little ones with me in the front. They had plenty to occupy them, as Mrs Trew and Anne had given them an I SPY book, a Ladybird book apiece and colouring magazines and crayons. We would miss the Trews and, I realised, the customers, despite their idiosyncrasies…

It was the beginning of October, not late September, when we'd intended to move, so we had to make the most of the daylight. However, we were still in Devon when the engine began spluttering. Overheating, was John's first reaction. He spotted a layby, and opposite – was it a mirage? – a *fish and chip shop,* lit up, in the middle of a row of other small shops which were obviously closed. We had come upon this little village – (we never found out quite where it was) by chance.

We parked in the layby, and John went over to the shop to buy our supper and to enquire if they had a phone so that he could call the RAC.

'We'll stop a bit further up the road, to eat our food, where there are no houses,' I promised the boys. 'Then you can get out and stretch your legs and bob behind a bush...'

We managed to cruise along perhaps two hundred yards, then the vehicle lights failed and the engine seized up. By torchlight, for it was now dusk, we opened up our newspaper parcels and scoffed the contents with our fingers dipping in and out. Then I poured tea from the flask into paper cups and handed three back to the boys.

'We can't get out with all this stuff jamming us in,' said a worried voice, 'and we want to – *go* – now we've drunk the tea…'

John had the solution–' you'll have to use the empty paper cups – then open the window…' He always deals with our dilemmas, I thought gratefully, when another voice called out, 'Dad, a paper cup isn't big enough…' (Please note, I know who it was, but I'm not saying!)

It was past ten p.m. when the RAC arrived: our directions had been rather vague, they said. A powerful beam illuminated the problem. The alternator had gone. 'Look, I'll charge the battery, that should get you home, but not tonight with no lights. Wait until dawn, then take it steady all the way,' we were advised by the mechanic.

We settled down as comfortably as we could, put our coats on and hoped for the best. John and I slept but fitfully. Gentle snoring from boys and Billow, then we shook with stifled laughter, as we heard Billow lapping water. From the goldfish bowl… I hope he doesn't swallow Goldie, I thought.

We were stiff and cold in the early morning, but the boys managed to shift the furniture in the back to open a side door, and stepped down to take the dog for a run in the field beyond the hedge where we were parked. Tiger had to make do with a litter tray in case he stalked off and we couldn't find him quickly. We were relieved the goldfish had survived the dog's thirst. Maff and Katy appeared to have had a good night's sleep!

We drank tepid tea and ate the ham sandwiches we'd reserved for breakfast in our new abode. But none of us were able to wash.

Well, we coasted carefully along and there were more mini-crises along the way, but I'll draw a veil over those. John had to phone the haulage company first thing to let them know we would not be in residence until late afternoon. They were not sympathetic, having planned to unload us early and then reload for another trip, later in the day. We were told we would be penalised, but were past worrying about that.

We arrived in Kent, travel-stained, and it was just starting to rain, as we looked out at our chapel, an imposing red brick edifice, built by local Methodists in 1884. It was surrounded then by a meadow starred with daisies, (where later a new estate would be built) with a village football pitch beyond – our boys would love that! The main feature at the front was a beautiful round stained glass window which we discovered beamed rainbow light to the gallery. John wisely didn't mention then, that along the far side was a graveyard, but all the ancient memorial stones had been laid flat, and this area we were bound to grass over. The windows along the chapel walls were typically ecclesiastical, long, curved, occluded glass, but difficult to curtain adequately. The entrance was not what we expected, John would make a splendid new door a priority.

The haulage men had decanted our furniture into the front garden, to pay us back for being late, and there was an overflow on the pavement, now getting wet. Our new neighbour came out to help.

'Your girls are waiting in the kitchen,' he told us. 'We had a key, so let them in. They've been worrying about you all day!'

We hadn't expected them until Sunday, so this was a wonderful surprise. Jo and Ginge had the kettle on and they'd been to the shop for milk and tea. It was quick hugs all round, and a chorus of Happy Birthday! to Ginge who was eighteen today, before we got down to business. 'We'll celebrate tomorrow,' we promised our lovely daughters.

The previous occupants had obviously departed in a huff judging by the terrible mess they had left behind. There were numerous letters (opened but thrown in a heap on the floor in the main room) from their bank, unpaid bills and threatening letters from the suppliers. I pounced on bottles of sleeping pills and anti-depressants and put them in a safe place. Worse was to be revealed, there were two bedrooms downstairs, designated for the girls (when home) and the three boys. There was a bathroom downstairs, and another upstairs – two more bedrooms led off the gallery, under the eaves, for John and I, Katy and Maff.

The girls' bedroom was filthy – our neighbours told us that our predecessors had kept two large dogs and eight puppies in there! We located the Dettol and cloths, fortunately the girls had turned on the immersion heater, so there was plenty of hot water. It was going to be another long night... Then in walked dear Jonathan who'd driven from Suffolk, where he now worked, to offer both moral and physical support. He is always so positive and cheerful!

The kitchen was the only room which had been fitted out properly. The drawback was the uneven floor. The dog owners had dug up a lovely brick path which encircled the chapel, and cemented all these bricks in place. We got wet muddy feet from trailing round outside, bringing in our goods.

Had we exchanged one disaster for another, we wondered?

Then I saw something which gave me hope for an uncertain future. There was a small room, which we thought would make a cosy dining room. With the long table, the settle, chairs and small dresser in place, this room would prove our refuge, and the sanctuary where I would write many stories. As we brushed away the cobwebs, gold lettering was revealed on the wall. This message must have comforted so many in times past. It read:

HIS MERCY IS EVERLASTING

Footnote

Although there was another defining moment to come (but that's a new story) I want readers to know that despite all the hard work ahead, we spent many happy years in our chapel. We became involved with village life, and the local school, made good friends, and I never stopped writing. We celebrated many family occasions there – the Scalectrix and the snooker table on the gallery were a big draw! – and weddings and anniversaries were a doddle, with so much space!

To end on a very happy note – Maff (now Matt!) chose to marry his Lisa there in the parish church this year. We still have strong ties to this special place.

The publishers hope that this book has given you enjoyable reading. Large Print Books are especially designed to be as easy to see and hold as possible. If you wish a complete list of our books please ask at your local library or write directly to:

Dales Large Print Books
Magna House, Long Preston,
Skipton, North Yorkshire.
BD23 4ND